About the Author

CEON is a queer Scottish author living in England, their first novel *The Condition: Impervious* was published March 2022, in the thriller genre at twenty-three years old. They have also been published in various magazines/zines for poetry and life stories. They aim for all of their books to have queer and mental health representation.

Allure

CEON

Allure

Olympia Publishers
London

www.olympiapublishers.com
OLYMPIA PAPERBACK EDITION

A CIP catalogue record for this title is
available from the British Library.

ISBN: 978-1-80439-355-0

This is a work of fiction.
Names, characters, places and incidents originate from the writer's
imagination. Any resemblance to actual persons, living or dead, is
purely coincidental.

First Published in 2023

Olympia Publishers
Tallis House
2 Tallis Street
London
EC4Y 0AB

Printed in Great Britain

Dedication

This book is dedicated to the sapphics, what a beautiful life it is to live, loving women.

Much love,
CEON

Acknowledgements

Thank you to my friends – Finn Robinson and Matthew Watson for always being there for me. Thank you to Poppy and Kittie for being the cutest fluffy family members (yes I am giving thanks to my cats). Special thanks to Elinor Prescott for lending her artistic skills for the cover typeface and to Lizzie Styles (@too.small.for.you) for her fantastic cover art.

Chapter One

Dominic is finally going away again with work, which means I can have the apartment to myself and invite someone over via the app 'Fun timz' – horrible name but it serves its purpose. Now, don't you worry, we're in an open relationship so it's not like I'm doing it behind his back. Open because we want only sex with others when he's away with work, rather than being poly or ENM and have relationships. He'll have someone in his hotel room and I'll have someone in our home, only women really; I'm with Dom after all and bless him but once you've been with one man, you've been with them all.

We live in a small town, so the selection of WLW is very modest, and even more humble than that when you're not looking for anything serious. I'll waste time swiping on the app before reverting back to the two same women I've met before; one that drives from a few towns over and the other that walks an hour to get here.

Tonight's swiping threw me off my game. Coming across Morana was exciting. She didn't seem real, but she had enough pictures to prove she wasn't a catfish. Her bio simply stating, maybe even daring:

'Let me have you.'

On any other profile I may have cringed, but on hers it proved more enticing. I figured she was probably passing through and not checking her app. There's not much worth staying here for, so there's no real pull for interesting people.

To my surprise: we matched.

While I pondered something witty to say, she beat me to the chase:

'Address?'

I knew this was almost too good to be true, but I couldn't help but take the risk.

Chapter Two

I put on a casual dress, mood lighting and set up some wine.

I opened the door to the most stunning person I'd ever seen in my life. She was stood right in front of me and I still couldn't believe she was real. Wearing a short blue lacy dress, her blonde hair braided like a crown atop her head, she smiled at me with a hint of menace, I must've been gawking.

"Come in." I held the door open for her. I sat on the couch. "Wine?" I turned to face her; she shook her head. "Oh, driving?"

"Something like that, yeah." She shrugged.

"Do you mind if I—?"

"Of course, whatever makes you feel good." I think I drank the glass quicker than I had poured it, I was struggling to keep my cool. She hadn't even sat down yet.

She stood over the couch and reached from behind to massage my shoulders, her touch was cold, but still started a fire under my skin. In that moment I just wanted to merge with her, it wasn't sexual, but I just wanted to be near her – at one with her. She worked her hands around my neck, gently stroking my throat with her thumbs.

I softly removed one of her hands, keeping hold of it in mine, standing and turning to face her. None of us moving our hands: mine holding hers and her other still lightly on my neck even while I turned. I looked in her eyes and started to lean in while holding her hand next to my heart. Hoping for a kiss.

Without separating, she stepped back and smirked.

Chapter Three

"Bedroom?" She darted her eyes to the stairs as if to ask. I attempted to answer but seemed to have forgotten how to breathe. Instead moving my head into what I hoped was a nod. She took me upstairs by the hand and positioned me standing in front of the bed. As if in a trance, I started taking my dress off as she stared into my eyes, there were no words, but she was in charge. I slid down one strap of my bra.

"Stop." I glanced up at her. "Lie down." I didn't know this woman – but I felt like I'd do anything for her. I floated back without looking away from her, kicking myself further up the bed closer to the pillows.

She crawled on top of me, an animalistic look burned in her eyes. Facing each other I lunged my head towards hers, desperate for her kiss, and with one arm she pushed me back down and giggled.

She gently kissed my shoulder, then the corner of my jaw. She hovered over my neck for what felt like forever, but in reality, was probably only a few seconds. Then she bit. She bit right into me. I felt the skin tear beneath her lips. My neck turned to fire, the pain was indescribable, I wanted to pull away but also didn't at the same time. It felt like I was dying, I felt with each pound of pain throbbing from my neck that a piece of my energy was taken from me. She reached down and grabbed my hand, letting me squeeze her tight and somehow – as strange as it was – this experience was more intimate than anything I'd ever been part of before. She bit into me and I liked it? Violence and kink were not regular things on my sexual radar.

She was on top of me biting harder and harder, until I passed out.

Chapter Four

I was woken up by the most delicious smell I'd ever experienced. I was in bed alone. I got up and felt as though I had floated towards the scent like a cartoon character would to a pie. Maybe Morana had helped herself and started cooking. Although when I reached the kitchen, no one was there, but the smell remained. I looked across the room and saw Dominic sitting on the couch playing a video game. He must've come home early, and Morana must've snuck out. Last night was like a fever dream, and I don't remember much of the night. I stared at the back of his head. *'Kill him,'* a voice that wasn't mine spoke to me in my mind. *'You'll know what to do,'* she continued. The familiarity of the voice reminded me of what little words Morana had spoken to me last night, her voice was unforgettable. Smooth, enticing, daring, commanding. My blood ran through my body like a shock, my hands started shaking. Obviously I didn't want to kill my boyfriend, but my body didn't get the memo.

He dipped his head upside down to look at me from the couch.

"Oh, hey." He smiled at me, he continued talking but I couldn't hear him, my ears were ringing, and I had gone into shell shock mode. Sprinting back up the stairs and locking the bedroom door behind me, I was understandably wigged.

I started to open the blinds so I could climb down the fire escape when she spoke to me again, *'I wouldn't do that.'* I ignored her and continued, I just wanted to run away, to get fresh air in my system. I couldn't be near Dom if I were going to accidentally kill him. The sun stung my skin but I took no notice, that is, until my arm started to smoke. *'No tan.'* A pang in my stomach threw me to the floor, my stomach felt like it was eating itself. Dom knocked on the door.

"Hannah, are you okay?" he asked worriedly.

"Eh, yeah I'm just not feeling well," I white lied, "can you leave some food behind the door? I need to be alone." I heard his feet tap down the wooden stairs, Dom was a great boyfriend, he understood and respected boundaries and was never upset when I needed time alone.

Eventually there was a knock on the door and I dragged my body across the floor, barely able to find any strength. I heard his feet shuffle away under the door. I opened it up and snatched the plate, locking myself in the room again. He had made me an omelette. I sat in the corner of the room, rolled it up in my hands – *'That's not what you need'* – and bit into it as if it were a fajita. My stomach growled and flipped as my body rejected the food nearly as quickly as it had entered. *'Ooh poor baby,'* she said with a hint of sarcasm. I lay there on the floor, my eyes welling up and my body feeling defeated. I wasn't going to cry but it instead seemed that my eyes were watering purely to blind me. *'You know what you need.'* I slapped my hand on the floor. *'Kill your boyfriend.'*

Chapter Five

I pushed myself up. My hand trembled as it reached for the door handle. Almost as if her words had taken me over. My hand got close, but I couldn't. I was still in a watery blindness, and I thudded my head against the door, fighting my body's urge to leave. *'Drain his body, your body will know what to do.'* I thrust myself away from the door so hard that I fell into the door to our ensuite. I sat there, head in hands, dizzy. While on the floor I caught a whiff of a faint version of the delicious smell. I opened the door and followed the scent to the bin and started digging, until I got to a bloody used tampon, my body went into overdrive, I shoved it into my mouth and sucked on it like it was a throat sweet. The crusty outer layer cracked off and melted like butter in my mouth. My eyes unblurred and the world became warm. The thought was disgusting, but the taste indescribable. Everything turned to saturate and my body buzzed.

When I woke up on the floor it was dark out. I took the opportunity to jump out the escape. Maybe a walk would help me. I touched my neck where she had bitten me but there was no mark, or at least I couldn't feel one. She hadn't spoken to me, and I would've thought she'd have something to say about me sucking on my own tampon, for sure a memory I'd love to erase, but couldn't get out my mind, the euphoric feeling it brought me. None of this could be real, could it? Morana was too beautiful to be real, and the events that followed from meeting her didn't make much sense. But this was also too lengthy and felt too real to be a dream.

I caught myself walking into the local club, maybe a drink would do me good. Before I knew it, I was surrounded by people, and the smell was back. The room was spinning, my mouth went dry. It felt as if my eyes were poking out of my head. I headed towards the toilet when a man approached me mumbling and grabbing my waist. With one arm I pushed him against the wall which made him laugh.

"Oooh yes, baby, I like it rough." What a pig. He should die, all men like this should die. Once again my body took over and I found my head moving in slow motion towards his neck before I was interrupted by a thud on my shoulder pushing me into the ladies room and up against a locked cubicle door.

"What the fuck are you doing?" The woman grabbing me sounded angry, but the expression on her face showed shock. "In public, are you insane? Imbeci—" She looked into my eyes and a dread flooded over her face.

"Excuse me, I just wanna get out please," a nervous voice muttered behind the door.

"We need to get out of here." The woman dragged me into an alleyway as far away from the club as her patience would allow her. "How long?" She finally let go of my arm. "How long since you were reborn?" she clarified.

"Since *what*?" I felt my face scrunch up.

"Am I being punished? Why has life got to test me like this?" She flailed her arms and spoke upward as if speaking to the heavens. She squished the bridge of her nose and sighed. "You don't even know what you are, do you?" A look of empathy snuck out for only a second.

A drunk group came stumbling and talking loudly. "We're going to mine."

"No, I need to go back to my boyfriend." She glared at me.

"And you have the urge to kill your boyfriend, correct?" How could she know that? "And I assume you don't want to?" I nodded. "Come with me." She grabbed my shirt between my chest, dragging me again and not giving me much option.

Chapter Six

We entered her flat, a dark high-ceilinged urban type building with exposed brick. The kitchen and living room were one room and there were three doors opposite the entrance.

"I didn't realise there'd be more of you," a man spoke up from the kitchen island, I noticed he was wearing some sort of medical bracelet.

"Yeah, me either," she responded while pulling me towards one of the doors.

"Who's that?" I asked as she burst the door open.

"Him? You don't acknowledge him, okay?" I nodded as she sat me on the bed.

"Woah, you're really beautiful." I realised aloud, taking her in properly for the first time. She rolled her eyes at me.

"You're just hungry." She tapped my shoulder in a patronising way then left the room.

She entered again throwing a bag of liquid at me. It was a blood bag, with the address of a hospital a few towns over. I placed it on the bed beside me, I don't understand why she would have that nor why she'd give it to a stranger like me. "Drink."

"You want me to drink the blood?" She picked up the bag and shoved it onto my chest.

"You've drunk blood before, haven't you?" I didn't want to remember sucking on my tampon, how would she know about that anyway? "I'm helping you here, even giving you my emergency stash, unless you want to kill people? Then that's a different story and you can get the fuck out of my home." I didn't understand what in the hell was going on. She snatched the bag from me and loosened the lid, taking a chug out of it herself, then shrugged and handed it to me. The smell, it was that same smell, I took a deep breath in, filling my body with the warmth that the smell brought. Then before I knew it my eyes were blurring while watching her as I necked the bag.

I woke up and could see light peering across the ceiling. I had slept in this woman's bed, Dominic must be worried sick, or maybe he slept on the couch not knowing I had left.

I moved into the open space. The man was sitting on the couch with his arm outstretched and the woman had her head seemingly buried into it. He noticed me and tapped her shoulder; she moved her gaze up to me and I could see more clearly that she was fully biting into him and he was just letting her. I felt woozy and fell to the floor. *'Why is she allowed to and you're not?'* She disconnected and pulled up a cloth bandage that was sitting crunched up on his wrist to cover the wound. They exchanged a glance and he stated, "I'll go out for a smoke" to the room. She gently squeezed his arm for his attention.

"Don't do anything silly, Daniel." And he dipped his head in response. She crouched down next to me and touched my hair. "Hey, we have an agreement." I didn't look at her. "He tried to end himself, so he doesn't have much care for his wellbeing—" She tapped my shoulder and I looked at her face. "And he lets me feed, and lets me stay here, and I try to help him find a reason to stay." I don't really know what to say. "This is what I do in every city I go to, it's how I get by." I rubbed my head.

"Why does she keep talking to me?" She looked worried.

"Hm, when your instincts try to take over, your maker can contact you." She grabbed my arm and pulled me onto the couch.

22

"Is she being helpful?"

"She wants me to kill my boyfriend." I shook my head. "I don't want to, but my body does, and her words just get me more rattled."

"Okay, try not to listen to her. You need to try and not get emotional, otherwise she'll pop up and try to ruin you." She tapped my knee. "Do you understand what's happened? What's happening?" I shook my head and she sighed. "Okay, this will sound weird but—" she tapped her fingers in a tickle across the back of the seat "—you've been turned into a vampire." I glared at her, I knew she was right, it made sense from what had been happening, but I still didn't expect the word. Although being a vampire altogether made no sense, I could sense she was a 'no time for this shit' sort of gal, even though she appeared nearly sympathetic in this moment.

"So, like I'm immortal now?" She let out a breath that was a low laugh.

"Not really; we don't age, and we can live forever, but normal human stuff can still kill us, plus the sunlight." She gestured towards the light beaming across the ceiling. "And if we kill a human from feeding, we lose our souls, and become demons, or more of one than we already were." Daniel walked back into the flat and went straight to the fridge without speaking a word. "Which means your lady is trying to sabotage you." Why would Morana want me to lose my soul? And why did the bad guy in my life have to be so hot and inviting? She stretched out and yawned.

"You haven't slept," Daniel stated, and she threw one hand out and shrugged. "Go to sleep, we'll be okay." She grabbed me by both shoulders and looked deep in my eyes.

"If you get even the slightest bit hungry, you come and get

me okay? If you hurt Dan, I will destroy you," she threatened.

She stopped in the doorway of the bedroom. "Araceli, by the way."

"Oh, Hannah." She was already halfway through closing the door when I responded. I walked over to the island and whispered to Daniel, "Are you okay? You're not being held hostage, right?" He chuckled.

"No, no, Araceli is great." He rolled down his bandage to reveal self-harm scars underneath the mark Araceli's teeth had left. "I'm suicidal." I just stared at her teeth mark. "But helping Araceli live gives my life a purpose, weirdly." I sat back in the chair just listening. "I guess that's why people with mental health issues get pets; in a way, I'm responsible for her survival."

Chapter Seven

I couldn't decide if Araceli was good or bad. Was she taking advantage of the vulnerable, or was she 'helping' them like she claimed? At the very least, Daniel believed she was helping, and that counts for some good, right? In some way it was intimate, they relied on each other to be able to live. But if she really didn't want to hurt people couldn't she just drink animals' blood like the vampires on TV?

It was night-time now. Araceli burst out of her room and threw a jacket at me.

"We're going out, got things to do." She rustled Dan's hair from behind him while he sat on the couch, which gave me a flashback of Morana and how one night that should've been fun, ended up changing my life forever, and I didn't even end up having any fun. She hugged him from behind. "Do you need anything?" He shook his head. "Stay safe." She led the way out of the door.

"So, are you like dating him or something?" I asked on the street.

"You never seen platonic love?" She judged.

"So, what are we doing?" I changed the subject.

"Getting you some blood." I stopped in my tracks.

"I'm not hurting anyone."

"Pfft, as if I'd let you near a human with your clear lack of impulse control." She grabbed my arm to drag me but I shook her off and followed anyway. "We're going to rob a blood donation van, you can drink from bags." I felt like her kid sister that she'd been burdened with babysitting. "You won't be able to bite without killing if she's in your head."

"Maybe I just don't want to be a vampire, I'll just not drink anyone's blood and die." That made her stop in her tracks this time.

"We can't do that, when we get starved our body takes over and we will likely kill, having no control or energy." She waved her index finger in my face. "If you want to lose your soul then don't waste my time helping you, I have my own life to look after."

"How do I stop Morana from messing with my head? You don't seem to have anyone bothering you."

"You don't, unless you think you can kill her," she scoffed. "And not everyone's maker wants to see them fail, mine didn't, but hers did." She shook her head. "Okay, so you keep them distracted outside of the van and I'll sneak in and steal some." She pointed at the van in the middle of a supermarket parking area. The two workers were standing outside already. I slowly approached them.

"Hey, you reet?" The male one spotted me first. Was it wise of us to go into this without a proper plan? What was I even doing assisting in a crime? "Can we help?" he nudged.

"Ehhhh—" Araceli slipped in behind the two of them "—I'm just a bit nervous around needles I guess."

"You want to give blood or whit?" He didn't seem to have patience even though there clearly wasn't much else for him to be doing.

Before I could think of saying anything else she popped out of the door, which the female one noticed.

"Hey! What are you doing?"

"Sin saber ingles." Araceli waved her arms in a cross, while nodding at me to leave while she had their attention. I ran and hid nearby, and after a few minutes she joined me.

26

I giggled at her.

"Good idea with the Spanish."

"Ah well someone needed to be useful, you had no clue." She nudged me, in a playful way.

We stopped to sit on a wall nearby and she took a deep breath in, staring at the stars.

"You said you had a platonic love for Daniel?" She continued staring at the sky. "But you mustn't have known him for long?"

"How long do you need to know someone to be able to feel close to them when they're the whole reason you're alive now?" I just watched her, watching the stars, and she smirked. "What makes you think 'not long' anyway?"

"His medical bracelet, he must have been in the hospital recently."

"He keeps that on as a reminder to himself, he can recover without me, they all can. But people tend to need something to pinpoint on, that's why lots of people claim their favourite celebs saved their life." She took another deep breath, this time closing her eyes.

"Does it hurt?"

"Does what hurt?"

"Becoming so close with these people, and knowing you'll outlive them?" She glanced at me then shrugged.

"It's just how life is, it's just the same as losing people while human; it hurts, but you learn to accept it." She started kicking her legs like a child. "Do you remember your last day outside in the sun?" I pondered for a moment then nodded. "Can you tell me about it?"

Chapter Eight

She told me about how her mother had been turned into a vampire shortly after she was born, and how she had killed Araceli's father almost immediately. Her 'tío' had chained her mother up in the basement and tried to 'help' her but she killed her husband, so her soul was gone. Although she had been raised by her 'tío', she never knew any of this until eighty years later, when she recognised her mother perfectly from the photos she had seen as a child, as evidently she hadn't aged to change. She said it made strange sense that they'd both end up vampires, as to be changed, you must have a certain quality, which no one really knows what it is but it's said that it makes a human's eyes glow and will make a vampire naturally magnetised to change them, almost as if it's their fate, written in the books. She said it was mystifying getting to know her mother for that brief meeting, and she even began imagining having some sort of life with her, until they discovered that they were at different sides of vampirehood. They still ran into each other every decade or so, and she said her mother holds on hope that she'll have lost her soul.

"It's weird, because we'll act as normal as a mother and daughter can in our situation, for say an hour, until—until she shows the loss of her mind, her soul, anything that would resemble who she really was and I'll never get to know that woman, only the demon that has stolen her body." It was strange to see someone so muscular, be so vulnerable, obviously she's a person with feelings like the rest of us, but originally she didn't seem to have the time for me.

"What about the men? You've only mentioned female vampires."

"I've never met one – they're pretty rare. The other micros I've met said—" she looked at my confused face "—micros; we call ourselves micro dosers, and you would be a baby because you're new, or sober because you can't drink from a human without killing."

"My baby," a voice from behind us chimed in.

"Morana." I thought I was saying it with dread but my tone came across more welcoming than I had intended. We turned around to face her and she walked towards me, putting her hands on my face, her hands warm and soft, almost comforting. She was here with another woman, another vampire.

"No creation of mine will be known as a sober; we'll fix you, baby." Araceli snatched her hands off my face and Morana took a step back giving her a sharp angry look. "Now you wouldn't be trying to steal what is mine, would you?"

"Leave her alone." Araceli stood up and made it so that she was slightly overlapping me. Morana rolled her eyes.

"Men—" she continued our conversation "—men think they're invincible, and men are always wrong; so usually they get themselves killed, or they lose their minds, anyway, eternal life looks so much prettier with all women, don't you agree?" Araceli folded her arms and huffed at her, trying to not let her address me. "Speaking of men, we were just going to yours actually." She peered round Araceli to look at me. "To meet your boyfriend." This made me stand up. Araceli threw her bag at the friend's head and tackled Morana to the ground.

"Go get your boyfriend, take him to ours." I stared at them wrestling each other on the ground, not wanting to leave. Two beautiful women on top of each other fighting because of you was probably something many people dreamed of, but I wished it wasn't happening, not wanting either of them to be hurt, even though one was threatening my boyfriend. "Fucking go, Hannah," she commanded agitated.

I ran.

Chapter Nine

I ran so fast. I thudded the door repeatedly until a groggy Dominic answered the door, hair in his face. He rubbed his eyes.

"Hannah?" He reached out to cuddle me, but I stepped out of reach.

"We need to go, you're in danger." Before even giving him a moment to process, I grabbed his hand and dragged him out of the door. It wasn't until we had got outside that he broke apart our hands and came to a halt.

"What the fuck, Hannah?" He threw his hands up. "Where have you been?" I put my hand out for him to hold it again.

"We really need to go."

"No, tell me what's happening!" It was weird to see him so demanding, as he was usually very passive, but I guess me disappearing for a day had stressed him out.

"Dom." I didn't know what to say, and before I knew it, didn't know what I was saying. "We need to break up." My seriousness made him take my hand and continue following without a word.

When we got into Daniel's, Araceli was already back, sitting at the island. She had a black eye and her cheeks were puffy. "Oh my, Araceli! Are you okay?" I ran towards her and put my hand on her cheek which made her flinch. She softly moved my hand off her face but continued to hold it.

"You should see the other guy." She smirked and shrugged. Daniel chucked her a bag of frozen peas which she put to her face then glanced back at Dom. "Glad you got him." He went red in the face and started marching towards us.

"Is this why?" He pointed at her. "Because of this *butch*?"

"Hannah, you didn't tell me your boyf' was a homophobe." She raised an eyebrow.

"He's not—" I shook my head. "You're not, don't be so rude." I pushed his hand down.

"I took a beating for this dude to rock in using slurs?" I didn't know what to say, or what to do. Dominic had never spoken like that, he was scared and angry but it was no excuse. I was so embarrassed.

"Can we talk?" he asked me, ignoring the existence of everyone else in the room. I led him to the bedroom I had slept in before. "You need to explain what in the hell is happening." I hesitated, I had no idea what to say. "Who are those people? Did you really just break up with me?" He ran his hands through his hair, stopping as if he was about to pull it all out.

"Yeah." His eyes popped. "We shouldn't be together any more." He grabbed my arm. "And the way you just acted in there proves me right." I pulled myself away from him.

"I just don't understand." He sighed. I walked away, leaving him in the room. I couldn't tell him the truth, and I didn't know what else to say.

Daniel and Araceli were quiet. Without speaking, I picked up a cloth and started cleaning scratch wounds on Araceli's arms, she whispered that I didn't need to, but I continued anyway.

Chapter Ten

I was awoken on the couch by a poke. I looked up at Dominic, and around to notice Araceli had left.

"I apologised to your friend, but she just grunted at me and went to bed. I'm making you and Daniel food." I looked over at Daniel who shrugged at me, and we watched as Dom helped himself to the kitchen utensils. It was light out; the sun was spraying golden trickles across the ceiling.

I sat across from Dom as he started prepping food, Daniel sitting on the single couch going back to a nap.

I'll just let him cook the food and say I'll eat it later or something. We were both quiet, maybe not to wake anyone, maybe because we didn't know what to say, but it didn't feel awkward. Dominic was good at that, making things feel natural, and last night had been a fluke that really wasn't him and I know he'd be upset about his actions, even if he weren't showing it.

As he was chopping food, he looked up at me to smirk, to say 'it's okay' with one look and no words, but instead a sliding, swishing sound of the metal of the knife hitting something it shouldn't pierced my ears. I closed my eyes and jumped off the seat, walking backward trying to stop myself from seeing.

"ARACELI," I screamed, but it was too late; I took in a deep breath, warmth hitting my chest, my mouth salivating. My body thudded against something and my mouth filled with beautiful sweet juices. It was warm in my mouth, and I could feel it setting my body alight. I could feel a lump between my teeth and

33

discovered when I bit harder: more of the juice came out. I could vaguely sense movement around me, and I couldn't hear a thing, that is, before her voice came. *'What is eternal youth worth when you can't enjoy it? Burdened with a soul, it's not you, it was never going to be you.'* I opened my eyes; I could see the back of a neck and a piece of wall. I could tell I was killing Dominic, and I knew I should stop, but it was just too good. Maybe I had never loved him, maybe I was always destined to kill him and that's why I was drawn to him before I had been turned, after all; Araceli did say that it was fate. I felt something slide under my teeth between Dom's skin and my tongue, it hooked into my cheek and pulled me back, causing something to schism in my mouth. Everything blurred and I found myself in the bedroom with Araceli without even having felt us move from the kitchen. I looked at her, her arms bulging, panting breath, she was in a sort of panic which usually I'd feel empathetic about but, instead, everything inside me wanted her. I stood on my tiptoes and tried to kiss her, which she dodged.

"Stop, you're high." I sat on the ground, why does no one want to kiss me these days? "The blood." She looked in my eyes. "Sorry." And the last thing I saw was her elbow rushing towards my face.

Chapter Eleven

I woke up with my head under a chin and above some boobies. Panic flooded over me as I instantly had a flashback to last night.

"Dominic," I gasped. This caused the arms around me to tighten and the legs next to me rustled like a grasshopper. "Did I kill him?"

"Your boyfriend is fine," Araceli answered. "Glad you've come down from the high." She started rolling out of the bed.

"He's not my boyfriend, we broke up." She continued walking out of the room and I followed.

She started digging through the fridge.

"Can you get the first aid box? It's under the sink." I started rustling through the cupboard while glancing around the room. "He ran away, but he's okay," she said over my shoulder while leaning in and grabbing the box. "Are you any good at sewing?" She raised the thread in front of me, and it was only then I had realised what she was doing. She was missing her index finger on her right hand, instead there it sat on the counter in a sandwich bag. I remembered a flicker of something breaking in my teeth.

"Shit." I stared at the scene in front of me. "I'm so sorry; I didn't mean to—" She had lifted the bag near my mouth to mimic shushing me with her finger, which made her cackle, but only made me feel worse.

"You weren't in control; it's okay, it can be sewn back on." She started to take the finger out of the bag. I looked around. There was a clear wet patch on the wall and the floor had been

35

mopped, it looked like Daniel had to clean up my mess. I put my head in my hands and let out a sigh.

"I'm so sorry; I'll leave, I didn't mean to put anyone in danger." Araceli paused and shook her head. I avoided her gaze out of shame, but she put her hand on my cheek and made me look at her.

"You are not dangerous; you're just new. You are staying. If I ever thought you'd be a danger to us, you wouldn't be here." Her hand dropped from my face and she continued stitching herself. "Now please feed yourself before our Daniel comes home."

My hands shook as I tried to drink blood from the bag, my chest felt woozy and I thought I was going to throw up, my head throbbed and the more blood I forced myself to drink, the clearer the events of the morning were, and I started to cry.

"I wanted to kill him, I needed to kill him." Araceli put her arms around me. "And I really wanted to make her proud." I was ashamed at the validation that I felt I needed from Morana, even though I didn't want it. I sniffled like a child. "Why have you been helping me?"

"One less soulless vampire out there, if I can prevent it then maybe that's the reason for this eternal life shit." I glared at her.

"It's not just that; if it was just that you wouldn't also be nice nor would you have shared some of your stories." She chuckled at me.

"Is it *that* difficult for you to believe that someone might just like you? I don't talk to other vampires often, so it's nice to have the conversations that I can't have with humans." She squeezed my knee. "It's hard, but you are good, I know you're good and you don't want to hurt anyone." We were sitting on the kitchen floor when Daniel arrived back home, I began trying to speak but he lifted his hand in a stop motion.

"Please don't apologise, I forgive you." He began putting his shopping away. "What are you going to do about him?" I looked at Araceli for an answer.

"No one would believe him if he said anything, who would believe vampires exist really?" Daniel snorted at her answer, but I guess that's how she'd managed living with humans all these years.

"You never think any of the people you stay with will try and prove it?" he asked.

"The mental health system sucks, if you have the slightest history of any mental health issue, they'd rather tick a box saying you're schizophrenic than just listen to you, sadly," she said with confidence, and he nodded in agreement.

Chapter Twelve

Morana saw me trying to kill Dominic; she knew I wanted to. So I had hopes that she'd leave him alone, if only to let me do it myself. Araceli had said nothing about me trying to kiss her, and I said nothing about her knocking me out, or the fact she had spooned me all night, even though I had lost it. I was in some form of disbelief that someone – who didn't even know me that well – would stick by my side after an outburst like that. Dominic sure ran away fast enough anyway. But now I had these two amazingly strong women both playing the angel and devil on my shoulder.

"I thought you said we didn't have powers?"

"We don't."

"Well, how did I overpower Dom? And even made it hard for you to remove me?"

"We're *addicts*, honey." She tapped my hand in a patronising way. "It's hard to stop an addict from getting what they crave." She squeezed my hand before putting hers back on her leg. "Besides, you didn't really think you could take me?" She nudged me over playfully which made me laugh. She really was a buff beauty and I don't think my urge to kiss her before was any off base, I just didn't notice until that moment. Weirdly from being out of my mind from drinking from Dominic, it brought my mind some sort of clarity. Maybe it's just because she'd shown me kindness, or helped me through this confusing time, although I didn't think I could love anyone while Morana had this hold over me. She thought that I was her property, and every time I'd been around her, even while hearing her voice, I had felt like she owned me. "Do you still love him?" Her words took me by surprise; I had been so caught in my own thoughts.

"I guess I never stopped loving him, things didn't change, but now the thought of him makes me scared." I tried to gather my thoughts. "And if there were a way we could coexist, I wouldn't want to." I looked down at my feet. "My desire to kill him in that one moment was so much stronger than any love I'd ever felt for him – so maybe I never really loved him at all." She squeezed my hand this time not letting go. "If I were destined to be like this, maybe my life before was nothing, that it meant nothing. It maybe wasn't real." She let air out through her nose.

"Don't try to be deep." She chuckled. "Your needs have changed, not your personality, though I suppose a change in needs also can end relationships," she pondered. "I had a love, once." She squished my hand with the rhythm of a heartbeat. "We grew up together, best friends, but at one point we both knew we loved each other, although internalised homophobia stopped us from ever admitting it back then." Her eyes started to water, and she took a deep breath. "She got turned, and as soon as she came to find me, she saw my eyes and couldn't help herself. We spent twenty years together as vampires before admitting our feelings for each other and becoming a couple. I sometimes think that if we never became vampires, we would never have ended up together." She shook her head and smiled as a tear rolled down her cheek. "We could've had a long time together, but she got killed in a turf war." I squeezed her hand back. "She died trying to protect humans; it's what we did back then." She told me about how there were groups of micros that would try to chase killers out of town, and how things had got out of hand.

Chapter Thirteen

The next evening I knew what I wanted to do. I got straight up and started aimlessly marching around town. It took twenty minutes before Araceli had found me, yanking my arm.

"What are you doing?"

"I'm going to find her and get her to leave." I shifted away from her. She snorted a little. "What? You used to do it!"

"Are you really that obsessed with her?" I rolled my eyes, she was just trying to deter me. "What would you do anyway?"

"Dunno, ask her to leave?" She stopped me in my tracks this time, looking me deep in the eyes.

"You really think she'd listen to you? She'd easily turn the tables and get you to do whatever she wanted." I shrugged.

"Then we kill her then." I started to walk away when she grabbed my waist, the touch gave me a tickle before she placed her other hand on me and threw me over her shoulder. "What the fuck?"

"You want to go at her without a plan? Let's go home and talk about it, see how you feel tomorrow." I tried to wriggle out, but her grip was strong and there was no use. I grabbed onto her arm for support, I felt disoriented being up this high looking at the ground. When I say grabbed, I don't mean fully; my hands were much smaller than her biceps. She had such big muscles, yet I hadn't seen her exercise once in the time I'd known her. I suppose she'd had a lot of time to work on them, to be able to get away with not exercising for a while, it's maybe all she'd done with her eternal life, I wondered if her life were to flash before her eyes, would she only see herself pushing up and down from the floor? And at that, I had no clue how many years she had existed for, she likely would've died naturally before my grandparents were even a thought.

She carried me right into the kitchen before putting me down, both hands on my waist. She stared into my eyes, her pupils throbbing, for a moment it seemed she was going to kiss me, the thought made me tingle a little. Instead she just sighed and booped the top of my head with her chin. *'If you want to see me, go to the wall from before,'* her voice intruded my brain, making me squish my eyes closed from the pain, almost as if she were starting a migraine. I went to the fridge to get a blood bag, I hadn't fed before I left as I planned it as a backup in case I couldn't find Morana, hoping she'd eventually talk to me and tell me where she was, which I guess worked. I took a gulp, only for the blood to make a lump in my throat, threatening to come back up. I put my fist to my mouth, forcing it down with a heavy swallow.

Araceli peered at me with worry. "You've had a taste now." She pulled her face into a side frown. "Your body knows what it's missing, and that's all that it'll want." She rubbed my back. "It'll be hard, but you can do it." I took a deep breath and tried to finish the bag.

"I need to make sure Dominic is all right."

41

Chapter Fourteen

She was reluctant to let me leave but eventually trusted that my guilt was stronger than my need to be close to Morana. I felt bad for lying, but technically she was right. I harmed Dominic against my will, and it was Morana's fault.

It was her friend who was waiting on me. A small woman, similar in size to me. Her face was beaten in, much worse than Araceli had been. A line that seemed to run under her eyes and across her nose, face swollen.

"Yeah, your friend's a bitch." She caught me staring. "Would've killed me too." I looked around eager for Morana's entrance. "No, I need to take you to her." She started walking in front of me, then stopped to glance at me as I wasn't moving. Would it really be a good idea to follow her to places unknown? I needed to trust that she'd take me to Morana. She gestured for me to follow, so I did.

We walked to a fancy hotel, or as fancy as you could get in our small town. I was taken aback, were these two vampires really staying in a fancy hotel all while killing people? What kind of opposite land were we in where the ones who killed live in luxury and the ones that didn't had to hide and scrape by?

Of course they were located on the top floor: the penthouse. Walking out into a huge open space, kitchen, living room, dining room with a spiral staircase in the middle of the room likely leading to a bedroom. I could hear something scraping above the ceiling, across my head and towards the middle of the room until *boomph,* a flood of navy blue, pastel pink and red so dark it was almost black came flooding down the staircase crackling and snapping with every step it hit. The lifeless body of a young man lay face up on the floor. The click clacks of high heels further attacked the previously battered staircase, and not before long, Morana was stepping over the body, blood covering her face. She spotted me and grinned, then shooed away her friend. She reached the body and grabbed a handkerchief out of his jacket pocket, using it to wipe the blood off her face before approaching me, rubbing my cheek with her thumb and then lightly kissing it like posh people in films do. There was so much light around her, so much sophistication, that it almost made me forget she had just killed a man and thrown him down the stairs. She was mesmerising.

"Hello," she smirked at me, noticing my eyes dart from the body and back to her. "I should've left you some, eh?" She ran her thumb across the corner of her mouth. She led me to the living room area, sitting on a large L couch and gesturing for me to sit next to her. I hesitated; I wasn't here for a gossip. "Sit." She rolled her eyes. Best to keep her happy for now, I figured, sitting next to her. She crossed her legs, her dress peering up showing that her heels were those ones that had the bits that looked like chokers for ankles, what are they called? I don't know.

"Could you maybe stop messing with my head?" I sounded shy and nervous. I didn't want to be, I wanted to be authoritative, but she still sent chills through my body. She put her elbow on the back of the couch and rested her head on her index and middle finger across the corner of her face.

"Did you ever think about how that might affect me?" She tutted. "You think I want to be brought into your brain purely because you're too useless to keep yourself fed?" She side eyed me. "You know." She paused. "I could keep you satisfied." She leaned in closer to me, using my leg to steady herself. I felt myself fill with cold sweat. I leaned in, her lips getting closer to mine, and she giggled. "You think I'd reward you for torturing yourself? Not likely." My heart sank as she tapped my leg and moved back to her original placement. She's such a fucking tease. I throbbed a little.

"You didn't ask," I said trying to pull myself together by changing the conversation. "And you just did it and left me."

"You know we don't have a choice in these things." She put her hands up. "I was only after a meal, but your eyes controlled the narrative." She wiggled my chin with her thumb.

"So you didn't intend to bite me? Or to even sleep with me?"

"Pfft, me, sleep with a human – never!" She scoffed at the absurdity. "Why do you think you're so drawn to me anyway?" I pulled away from her, looking around the room. "It's because deep down you know you want this." She rested her arm on the back behind me. "Listen, it doesn't make sense to ignore nature, it's what you are—" I shook my head "—did you ever think maybe we are the good guys and your friend is the bad one?" I stood up, Araceli had looked after me, and she didn't kill people, I couldn't believe Morana was trying to take this route. "She nearly beat Merripen to death, you saw her face." She pointed towards the door. "It took me pulling her off of her to snap her out of her rage, she evidently isn't the saint she claims to be, Hannah." She was protecting Dominic, and would killing a soulless vampire even be a bad thing?

"Why don't you just leave?" I flailed my arms in frustration. "Find something else to do rather than torment me."

"Aw, but where is the fun in that?" Sharing a troublesome smirk. "You can either master being sober, or you can be who

44

you're meant to be, what comes naturally." She stood up, making me want to edge to the door. "But as long as you keep getting yourself into situations of instinct, or physical takeover, then I'm going to stay as your mind begs my attention."

I got to the door and put my hand on the handle. She only smiled and daintily waved at me, not even making an effort to stop me from leaving. I even walked by Merripen in the lobby and all she did was watch me leave. What a strange interaction. As probably planned, Morana had planted a lot of questions in my mind. I didn't really know anything about this vampire stuff, although I was sure that in some way Morana was bad, based purely on the fact that she bit me and left me on my own, but that didn't exactly mean that Araceli was good or telling any truth either.

Chapter Fifteen

It was still pitch black outside, so I figured I should actually visit Dominic, then I wouldn't have to feel as bad about lying to Araceli. While walking, I tried to make sense of the experience I had just had. How did I go into that hotel frustrated by Morana only to leave confused and a little horny?

Who on earth were the ones in the right here? Was my inability to control myself really the reason that Morana wouldn't leave? Obviously I knew killing was wrong, but why would something so natural have to be avoided? Everything in my body needed to kill, or at the very least, get blood directly from a living being. I was even rejecting the bagged shit. But if Morana were to just shut her mouth, I may actually be able to learn to micro dose like Araceli does. Also, I really had no idea that the hotel was *that* fancy, our little town really doesn't have any right to have something so upscale.

Other than killing people, Morana didn't exactly act how I'd imagined someone without a soul would act, but maybe that was part of her game, to try and make me question Araceli and our apparent shared morals.

Coming up to the door was weird, having to knock on where I had lived for years. Dominic opened, glanced at me.

"No," he adamantly announced and started closing the door again. I put my foot in the way, and he was careful not to hit it.

"Come on." I pushed the door back open. He disappeared

out of sight behind the door, still holding it ajar with one of his hands. He then placed two hip length sports bags that had been filled to the brim in front of me.

"I've packed most of your clothes, if you want anything else you can text or something," he continued trying to close the door before eventually stopping to match my gaze. I saw a bandage on his neck, held onto his skin by microporous tape. He sighed. "I left for a week and came back to you having become a druggie." A week? I thought he had come back early, unless I had been unconscious for that whole time? I can't believe he thought I was on drugs, like had he not known me all these years at all? At least he didn't think I was a vampire, somehow it felt like he was being much more rational than me. But it still hurt to know that he thought this is what I had become: hooked on drugs, so crazy to the point of attacking and biting him. I didn't know what to say, I just looked down at my feet. "Goodbye, Hannah." And he closed the door.

Buzz.

Buzz.

One of the bags was demanding my attention. Inside wrapped up in a hoodie was my phone. The screen filled with notifications from friends and family. All pretty much saying the same things like 'what happened?' Or 'are you okay?' – this all being in reaction to Dominic having changed our relationship status on social media and no one having heard from me in days. Multiple missed calls from my work, I assumed I didn't have a job any more. I didn't reply to anything, I didn't even know what I would say and maybe it'd be best if I just disappeared.

I chucked my phone in the river on the way back to Daniel's.

Chapter Sixteen

I got in and dropped the bags to the floor. Araceli came out of the bedroom to query the thump they had made. She took one look and speedily gave me a tight squeeze.

"That must've been difficult." She let me go. "Not just carrying them with your little arms." She winked playfully and I smirked at her. I knew she was being genuine before, now she was just trying to lighten the mood. I faded off to the couches, Daniel didn't seem to be in sight. Araceli sat beside me giving me a blood bag. "He's back working now, he's doing better, won't need me for much longer." She sighed with relief, but there was also something tense about her. I drank.

"How did you do it?" I took a sip. "When Dominic was bleeding, how did you not want to kill him?" I put the tip in my mouth.

"Of course I did," she said sincerely, "but also it's not like he looks like a walking steak to me – not everyone wants him." I don't know why but this made me laugh, causing me to spit some blood onto my lip. "You spilled." She curled her index finger under my chin, moving my face to look at her, slowly inching her face towards me, until her soft lips were on mine. I leaned into it, I kissed her back. She licked from my bottom lip to my top, also tasting the blood I had spilled on myself. She separated our lips and put her forehead against mine, our noses touching in what I imagined to be a heart shape. "Is this okay?" she whispered. I put my hand on the back of her neck and threw myself back into her kiss, putting myself on her lap and my legs around her waist and without breaking our make out she lifted me, moving up from the couch, and into the bedroom, gently putting me on the bed, holy shit it was hot. We stared at each other deeply as I sat on the middle of the bed and she stood overshadowing, both calculating what was about to happen, and if it was *really* about to happen. I made the confirming move and pulled off my shirt, she copied the motion climbing onto the bed to join me, I put my hands on both sides of her face and kissed her. I climbed around her so that she was lying and I was above her, she put her massive hands around my waist and I took my bra off. She licked up from my stomach to in between my boobs, then grabbing and kissing each of them. I pulled on the bottom of her sports bra and she pulled it off. A chill ran up my spine. We rolled around making out, me rubbing my knee gradually up her legs, right to the top. She wriggled her trousers off, and I stood and took off mine. She picked me up again and placed me on the pillows, brushing my hair out of my face for me. "Do you want to do this? Is it okay?" she asked moving her hand from my hair to my cheek, rubbing gently. I nodded frantically.

"Please."

Chapter Seventeen

I don't know if it was becoming a vampire or if it was the fact I had been waiting so long for a woman's touch, or maybe it was just Araceli, but my God that sex was freeing. I woke up in her arms again, for someone so tall and strong, she was extremely gentle and thoughtful. Weird to think how she went from not having any of my shit to whatever this was. Her hug was comfortable, warm, but also having her touching me still sent a buzz through my body. She made a happy hum in her throat and squished me more.

"Morning." She nudged her chin on top of my head.

"Hey." My heart fluttered. She ran her thumb across my back. It had become dark again and I think we had spent most of the time awake, having fun. "By the way, have you spent your whole eternal life just working out?" She didn't open her eyes but she giggled and nudged my shoulder with her fist.

"Well, you can't sleep the whole time the sun is out, what else am I supposed to do?"

"I don't know; read a book, binge TV?"

"Oh I don't have thoughts for TV—" She kissed me on the lips then continued like it was nothing "—but maybe I could've invested in a good book." Her body close to mine, her breath on my face, it was still making me wet. I never imagined myself being attracted to a strong woman, but she really is a buff beauty, and she certainly knew what she was doing. She took a deep breath in, sniffing the air. "Daniel's home." She opened her eyes looking into mine. "I guess I should feed." I squeezed her arm.

"Do you have to leave?" I felt so needy but being wanted was nice and the physical contact was welcome.

"I'd love to stay and cuddle," she said while unwrapping herself from my grip and getting up, "but last night was a lot." She glanced at me while getting dressed. "Both emotionally and physically, so I need to feed to stay in control." She leaned over and kissed me on the forehead before leaving the room.

I starfished in the middle of the bed, smiling at the memories of last night. At some point falling back asleep.

I was woken up by Araceli all dressed up wearing a button up shirt and Harrington jacket. She was drowned in a perfume that smelled like woodland.

"You're all dressed up?"

"Sherlock." She rolled her eyes. "The three of us are going out tonight, you need to eat and get dressed." She took my hand and guided me out of bed, kind of how a prince would escort a princess downstairs. Before pulling me out of bed, I paused. Last night was undeniably beautiful, and I do trust Araceli, but I still have questions floating around from my visit with Morana.

"What happened when I went to collect Dom? When you were fighting?"

"You want to know?" I nodded and she took a seat next to me on the bed. "Well, I'm not proud." Her leg jittered. "I was only trying to hold them back, so that you could protect him, so that I could protect you both but I stopped paying attention." She turned to face me. "I kind of flashed back to the turf war days and took it too far, I really hurt the ginger." She was looking down at her hands now, so I put mine on hers. "I didn't mean to, and I feel awful, obviously I don't believe violence is the answer, and have only ever resorted to it in the extremes through the years but the soulless grind my gears, I just don't understand how they can do what they do, and not have morals and only care about themselves – it makes me angry how they take lives simply because they like a taste."

"It's okay, you didn't finish it, you had control and that's what matters." We did a kind of melting hug. "Thanks for being honest."

"Always," she said rubbing my back, "why'd you ask?"

Hmph, I decided to tell her the truth. I don't think she'd ever had ill intent with me. I told her everything that happened in the hotel.

"Are you angry?" I had moved to rest my back on the headboard of the bed. She scooted over and lifted my outstretched legs onto her basket crossed ones.

"No, of course not, you're a grown woman. You can make your own decisions." She started rubbing my legs, only making me want to take our clothes off again. "Obviously I want you to trust me, but it's a weird situation and you would never have been prepared for becoming a vampire, so I'm kind of glad you went out to make your own truths about it." She crawled up closer to me, sitting over my legs and playing with my hair. "I'm thankful you didn't get hurt." I grabbed her shirt and pulled her in for a kiss, which she didn't object to. Then before pulling away tapped her chin on my hair. "Right, let's get ready to go."

Chapter Eighteen

I decided to wear a playsuit, simple, easy, smart. When I exited the room Araceli pretended to fan me off before throwing me a bag. Daniel came out of his room, hair slicked back, white shirt and a sports jacket, doing a little dancey spin to which we both applauded.

While walking outside, Daniel took the lead, Araceli outstretched her arm, clasping and unclasping her hand, non-verbally asking for mine. I took her up on the request, placing my hand in hers. I had to stop in my tracks. My brain had flashed back to Morana biting me and grabbing my hand, a cold sweat flushed my body and my neck set aflame. I rubbed where she had bitten me and then continued on.

"Where are we going anyway?" Daniel slowed down to walk in line with us so he could hear me, glancing at us holding hands then gazing off in front of us.

"To the club." I stopped in my tracks.

"Is that a good idea?" I asked.

"Amar, you'll be fine." She put two hands on my face. "We'll look after you." She jolted my arm to keep me moving. "It'll be best to have you get used to being around groups sooner."

We got into the club, music blaring, lights creating a multicoloured thunderstorm, and the ambrosial smell of warm blood cramped into one space. A world of overstimulation. I grabbed onto Araceli's arm with both my hands while she ordered drinks and squeezed tight. I was so distracted that I didn't even think twice about her ordering drinks. She handed me a bottle and I examined the label 'bistecs altos'.

"It's dark Spanish beer – high in iron, so we can drink it and it won't make us sick." She leaned over for me to hear her. Although I was terrified of snapping and attacking innocent people, I felt safe with her. I had never had a romantic relationship with a woman before, I never imagined it could be like this. Daniel coaxed us onto the dance floor and we all did goofy dances in a circle, even causing me to giggle and almost forget we were surrounded by what was essentially food. "Just keep yourself distracted," she told me, squeezing my arm. Daniel left off for the toilet and Araceli grabbed both sides of my waist and danced with me in a little wiggle that didn't go with the music at all, but we were both happy in the moment, getting to be together.

"So, what is this? What are we?"

"Well, what do you want us to be? Casual? A couple?" She flashed a big smile at me. "Hannah, can I please be your girlfriend?" My heart skipped; I couldn't believe that in all this madness I had met someone like Araceli.

"Yes." She lifted me up and kissed me. In that moment it felt like the whole room had melted away, it was only us. She spun me around. Eternal life seemed more survivable if I had Araceli by my side, keeping me out of trouble, making my heart flutter, having great sex. Living forever in darkness and drowning in my addiction – there could still be light, a flicker of happiness through the possibility of love. If we didn't run into trouble, I had the opportunity to live the rest of my life with a beautiful woman who could make me happy, but there would always be the grey sky that is: Morana. Not only with the constant torment and temptation that she drives to try and make me kill, but also the part of me that wanted her, and the never knowing if that desire was due to us being connected by her making me a vampire, or if it was something more genuine. And if it were genuine for me, would it be for her? Or was she just preying on my feelings and confusion.

Another hand peeling mine from Araceli interrupted our moment.

Chapter Nineteen

Who would be the typical person to interrupt a happy moment for me? Morana. Araceli puffed out her chest and stood between us. I leaned into her and whispered, "Just let her. If we keep her happy, maybe she'll leave us alone." Her shoulders dropped. She pulled me on the waist and kissed me on the cheek while giving her the side eye. Morana put her hand out like a posh girl expecting it to be kissed. I took her hand and she put her arms over my shoulders, in a slow dance type position.

"So, you two are together now?" I nodded. "That's boring." She rolled her eyes and separated. Slowly moving her arms in the air and wiggling her hips, moving to the floor slowly in a 'slut drop' fashion. "Why would you settle for hard work and seriousness?" She pulled me by my waist, looking into my eyes and putting her thumb on my lips. "When you can let go, be free and have fun with me?" Although she had up to date seduction moves, it was clear these two women were certainly from another lifetime, both jumping straight to the conclusion that monogyny is the only option. And you may be saying, 'Oh but, Hannah, isn't that what you just agreed to?' Well no, it's a conversation to be had later to set boundaries and expectations, a little too awkward to define in the middle of a dancefloor. Besides, I'm not sure how likely it'll be for me to come across another vampire that I'd want to sleep with or even have a relationship with. "Your girlfriend is staring." I looked behind me, she was dancing with Daniel, eyes burning on us.

"She's being protective, doesn't that prove that—" I was interrupted by someone slapping themselves into me, in a hug, parking my head beside her shoulder, right next to her neck. I gagged trying to reject taking in a whiff. I pushed her away and she stumbled to the ground, clearly drunk.

"Wow." She flailed her arms. "I was just excited to see you, Dominic said you broke up and you were unwell." She got up and dusted herself off. "No one has heard from you; what the fuck, Hannah?" She wiggled her index finger while approaching me again, only waving around her smell some more. My mouth watered, my vision blurred, I could feel myself filling with heat, I was so unjustifiably angry, and hungry. I started to hyperventilate before my body lunged towards where she was. A hand slipped into mine and started pulling at me. I followed where I was being led, while still not being able to see. Cold air smacked my face and I was placed with my back against something solid, which I slid down putting my head between my legs still struggling to catch my breath. Two hands softly lifted my face up and I felt a forehead against mine. Breathing loud enough for me to hear, I matched my breath to the pace and gradually my eyes unblurred to show me Morana.

"You were having a panic attack." She pulled away and sat in a squat, not touching the ground.

"Don't you want me to kill people?" It made no sense that she'd drag me out right when I was going to do exactly what she wanted.

"Babe, I don't want you to expose our existence, I'm not stupid." She smiled at the ground. A drunk man stumbled through the alleyway and my senses turned to a migraine haze. Morana rubbed her forehead clearly feeling my desire for a kill. "Hey, you! Do you want a sexy time?" He floated over and she grabbed his arm and put it under my chin. I looked at him, he was staring right through me, clearly blackout drunk. Do people that purposely get like that even deserve to live anyway? Of course they do, my brain was just trying to find any justification for killing, as my whole body wanted. She was staring at me and without breaking eye contact: she put his arm in her mouth, bit down, and started drinking a little, then thrust it towards me, some blood sliding out of the wound she had just made. I pushed my back into the wall as if I pushed hard enough it might fall through but it didn't help and the smell was too much, too close. I gave in. It was warm where her mouth had been, maybe this would be the only way our lips would actually meet. She put her hand on the back of my head and brushed my hair with her hand. "Good girl." Knowing I had pleased her only made me want to bite harder, to give in to my need. "Right, stop." She tapped my shoulder, but I didn't listen. "Stop, stop, stop." She pulled the arm away from me, making my teeth rip skin. The guy fell to the floor, grunting a little, but I could tell he had no idea what was going on. It felt like my eyes were going to pop out of my head, like I had just been slapped across the face, a thrill ran through my body making me buzz. I turned to look at Morana who was on top of the guy, head buried in his neck. Snapping her head up and taking a deep inhale, she returned to my level, wiping blood off her mouth with her hand, then mine with her thumb. "Better?" I nodded, not really understanding what had happened.

Thuds echoed through the alleyway and Araceli ripped Morana up grabbing her by the straps of her dress.

"What the fuck did you do?" she demanded, looking from her to the body and back.

"Oh that?" She stayed calm. "We just had some fun." Araceli grabbed tighter. I jumped to my feet and rustled myself between them.

"Stop, she helped me." I stood in between the two of them, Araceli still holding her up behind me.

"Oi! You!" a stranger's voice shouted from the darkness of the entrance of the alleyway, followed by a blur of high vis.

Chapter Twenty

It all moved rather quickly, but there was a bit of shouting while two police officers cuffed us all. I never paid attention because my first thought went to the body on the ground that had disappeared when I tried to glance at it. We tried to argue with the police, telling them that there was no issue; but they didn't listen. They took us to the station and prepared to put us in holding cells. Uncuffing me and Morana in front of one door as they started taking Araceli in another direction.

"Woah, you're putting them together?" she objected.

"Hey, this is a misunderstanding; we're all friends." I nudged Morana to get her to agree.

"Hm, I wouldn't claim that, I'm not going to lie to a police officer, Hannah." She smirked. They put us in our walled cell, and the officer explained.

"The big one had her in a threatening position, we're just going to check your backgrounds and let you cool off, if nothing comes up, you'll all be free to go."

The room was a solitary concrete space, certainly not made for comfort. The light squares built into the ceiling, projected a sickening yellow glow. The seat was an outstanding piece of concrete attached to the wall.

"How do you feel?" Morana spoke first. "Close your eyes, take a deep breath." I did, the room felt fuller, calmer. I opened my eyes and the lights rang in my ears. "Don't feel that pain any more, do you?" I actually felt full for once. I didn't notice before but drinking from the bags had left me feeling like I was holding my breath, that my body was only just scraping by with what it had. Although I didn't want to give her the satisfaction of my answer, I could tell she knew.

"Can't you see she'll look after me? We'll make sure I won't go hungry, so you don't have to stick around to make sure I don't bother your head."

"NO," she raised her voice. "I am responsible for you," she said in a softer tone, as if she were letting herself down by uttering the words. For the first time, she had actually sounded genuine.

"Well, I don't want to kill anyone, so there's no use in you staying here."

"I am entitled to my opinion you know, she thinks I'm bad because I think you should kill? Well, I say she's bad for making you fight against who you are, which is clearly causing you pain." We both sighed and sat next to each other in silence.

After a chunk of time in the quiet, I had a realisation.

"Wait, how will the police check your backgrounds? They'll notice you're a lot older than you look?"

"Well, I can't speak for your *bodyguard.*" She raised an eyebrow. "But I have a background set up for this kind of thing."

"What about the guy?" She looked confused. "Didn't you—" I looked around the room and whispered, "*kill* him?"

"Ah, yes, Merripen." And that was that – she didn't elaborate.

There wasn't a clock in the room, so there was no way of telling how much time was passing, but I think we were in there a good few hours before getting let out.

We got pushed outside, no one really said anything to us. The clouds were whitish grey. Before anyone could speak, Araceli

61

exited the building instantly grabbing me for a hug, my head fitting perfectly under her chin.

"Fuck." She separated. "We won't make it back before the sun." She turned towards the left. "Do you know anywhere dark we can spend the day?" There was nothing there, and if there was it was highly unlikely they'd let people in all day or even have blinds closed during the light.

"Stay with me," Morana chimed in. Araceli shook her head. "It's that or burn?" Araceli groaned but she knew we didn't have much choice.

Chapter Twenty-One

She led us up the spiral staircase into a bedroom and gestured her hands towards the bed.

"Okay, where will you be sleeping?" Araceli asked.

"This is my room." She put her hands on her hips.

"Where is the other bed then?" she asked further.

"What other bed?"

"What about Merripen? Where does she sleep?" I joined.

"Merripen?" She snorted. "You think I share a hotel room with my employees?" I thought Merripen was her friend? What work would she possibly do?

"So one bed?" She nodded at me.

"That's not happening, guess you'll sleep on the couch," Araceli added and Morana tutted.

"You can sleep on the couch, I'll keep our Hannah warm." Araceli rolled her eyes and huffed.

"How about nightwear? I can't really sleep in this." I gestured to my playsuit.

"Do I look like the sort of person that owns casual clothing?" She acted offended. "I'm sure Hannah will be happy to sleep naked next to me anyway." She winked at me. Araceli shaking her head behind her. "Or if you're boring, I'm sure the hotel has robes?" she reassured.

"You can wear a robe, cuddle into me on the couch, I'll stay awake – make sure she doesn't try anything."

"For the two oldest people I've ever fucking met, you both bicker like little children." Why couldn't they just be mature

63

about the situation?

"Oh, only for you Hannah," Morana joked. "You know, I can't believe the three of us are in the same room – next to a bed – and we're not fucking it out?" Forget bi panic, welcome bi excitement. I looked at Araceli with hope and excitement and she shook her head – shot down. "Think of all the tension we'd remove if we had sex." A threesome with the two most beautiful and alluring women I'd ever met; and Araceli was too stubborn. Or what I should say is that she was more set in her morals, which was admirable. Whereas I was happy to throw mine out the window for a morning, purely to fulfil a fantasy, to have some fun.

"Hannah, she's a soulless, we can't trust her," she said moving towards me.

"Wow." She raised her eyebrows judgingly. "I did not realise people still believed in that folklore bullshit, wait—" She gasped and giggled in realisation. "Does that mean you think I *actually* have no soul?"

"Well, you do kill people." I shrugged.

"I mean, didn't we all lose our souls in becoming vampires?" She sat on the bed. "Anyway – if you believe in God – do you think she made vampires to test us? Or maybe she did it to control overpopulation on her beloved earth." She tapped her index finger to her head, like the meme.

"*She*?" Araceli rolled her eyes.

"You really think a man has the ability to have all these people desperate to do everything that he asks?" She tutted. "I don't think so."

Araceli ignored her and burst through the door to the ensuite and popped out with a robe placing it on my chest holding it until I took it in my hands, turning me to leave the room. I looked back at Morana who wiggled her fingers in a wave.

Chapter Twenty-Two

I woke up, head on Araceli's lap on the couch.

"It's dark now, get dressed." She looked exhausted. She really didn't trust Morana. I got ready and we left without any sight of her.

"She's so desperate for your attention and you just give it to her, it'd be sad if she wasn't evil," she jibed, I tried to ignore her pettiness.

"Do you really think the soul thing is real?" Probably not the best question to ask when she's tired and angry, but I wanted to know.

"Yeah." She put her arm around my neck draping her hand over my shoulder.

"It's just, apart from killing people obviously—" I glanced at her but she showed no expression, only looking forward at where we were walking "—she doesn't seem to act outrageously."

"Maybe that's what she wants you to think?"

"But she could've left us to die in the sunlight, we'd be two obstacles out of her way." She only took a deep breath in which told me she was done with the conversation. So we continued home in silence.

When we reached inside, Araceli was just about to lead into the bedroom.

"Can we talk?" She turned back to look at me and wrapped her arms around me, kissing me on the lips.

"Yes, my girlfriend?" she said in a sort of exhausted sigh.

"About that actually." She looked worried but still held me. "Non monogamy, it's what I'm used to, what I'm comfortable with."

"So, like dating other people?"

"Yeah, possibly, depends what fits me and that person." She nodded in understanding.

"Whatever makes you happy."

"But what about you? You should be happy too."

"You make me happy, and you being happy and comfortable is good for me." She squeezed me before starting to walk towards the room again. "Han, this isn't about *her*, is it?" She said it as if it were dirt in her mouth, and it wasn't even her name.

"No, she doesn't even like me like that, but if she did, I'd want the option to explore whatever it was." She shrugged and entered the bedroom just as Daniel was leaving his.

"Hey! What happened?" He sat down on the single couch and I sat on the large one, telling him about the police, but not too much about Morana, instead just saying we had had a disagreement with another vampire – a stranger.

Chapter Twenty-Three

"Don't you think I could try micro dosing?" She shook her head at me.

"You can't control yourself, just drink from the bags."

"How will I ever learn if you don't let me try? The bags make me feel sick, Araceli."

"Do you really want to risk killing some innocent human?" She handed me a bag with force. "You're an addict, it's in your nature to kill."

"And what excuses you?" She gripped onto the counter.

"I've been alive a lot longer than you, Hannah, I've had time to practise, can you please stop questioning me for once?" We had been living a sort of passable domestic life the last month since that night in the police station, but in the last few days we seemed to have started bickering a bit. At first she had kept me in with cuddles and sex, and even letting me show her TV, but the thought didn't pass me that she was just trying to keep me inside, locked away. I know she's only being protective though.

This was my post bed meal. Last night I had a dream about Dominic, I only remember flashes of it, but I had been filled with the overwhelming need to check up on him. I forced the bag down and grabbed my jacket heading for the door, when Araceli grabbed me, holding me back.

"I'm going to see Dominic; I just need to get something off my mind."

"No." She didn't just? I?

"Fuck off, Araceli." She let go of my arm and watched me walk out of the flat. I couldn't believe she was trying to bark commands at me.

Chapter Twenty-Four

The door that was once ours was now a stranger to me. It had been nearly two months since I lived there, since that night Morana came along, and now everything had changed – including me.

I knocked, half expecting him to not be in.

"Oh, hey," his joyless tone came from behind me, he was carrying a supermarket bag in one hand and jingling his keys in the other. I stepped out of the way to let him unlock the door.

"Can we talk?"

"Come in." He pushed the door with his foot to hold it open behind him for me to enter. Nothing had really changed in the room, other than photos of us that were gone. Not surprising as I didn't claim any furniture, so why would he need to get rid of it? He put the bag on the kitchen counter and moved to the dining table where I sat across from him. His neck had fully healed.

"I'm sorry." His eyes darted away from me. "I realise I never apologised, and that's not okay." He nodded, avoiding eye contact. "I'm doing better now, I've stopped the—" I paused "— eh, *drugs*. And I've started to gain control again." He rubbed his neck where I had bitten. "Are you okay? How have you been?" I reached out to touch his hand, which he flinched away from.

"I—" He sighed. "I accept your apology, and I appreciate—" He stopped. "I'm glad you're recovering, but I don't think we're really in a place for chit-chat." He stood up.

"Oh, okay." I got up too, heading for the door.

"Thank you, though." He closed the door behind me.

Although weird, I did feel better from seeing him. It seemed to fill whatever had been nagging at me before, and he was right anyway, we shouldn't really be reconnecting, I don't want to be putting him at risk, or to be needing to explain vampirism to him. I guess, I just – for a moment – fell back into my human self, the habit of being with him and trying to look after his needs. It's not as if all of our history just disappeared even though my actions made a good job of trying to make it all burn down. I'm glad I got to apologise, and I hope in some way it helped him. I didn't want our relationship to finish on such a violent note.

Chapter Twenty-Five

When returning home, I was instantly greeted with a hug, and head bonk.

"I'm sorry – I didn't mean to speak to you like that."

"I know, it's okay but we need to be more aware of each other's boundaries."

"Uh-huh." She squeezed me in a sway. "We need to talk about something." She put me at arm's length. "Daniel can cope on his own now, and I've been here long enough." She took a deep breath. "So it's time for me to move on elsewhere." Leave? Would Daniel really be okay without the company? "And I'd love for you to come with me, we can continue our domestic bliss." I couldn't believe she was saying these words after the last few days we've had, fuck bliss, it was more of a domestic trap.

"And we'd find two humans in another city?" She didn't seem to understand the question. "To micro?" She squeezed the bridge of her nose.

"Han, I just don't think you're ready for that, but we can work on it in the future." I really loved the vote of confidence. "I want to continue living with you, you know I love you, Hannah, please think about it; I don't need an answer right now."

There were so many things to factor into this. Although I hadn't had any contact with family or friends in this time, I still wasn't sure I was ready to leave my hometown and them behind while we were all still alive, while I could still pass for the age I was meant to be. Although even if I wanted to, I doubt she'd let me have any close relations with any humans.

That morning we cuddled as we always did, her lying down arm around me while I used her torso as a pillow, but instead of comforting and warm as it once had been, it felt like a cage. Waking up that night didn't prove to be much better. I still had questions and all sorts of thoughts floating round in my mind, things I knew would make Araceli unhappy.

"Why don't you think I'm ready?"

"What? Not even a good evening? I just woke up, Han." She rubbed her eyes.

"I need to know."

"You don't need to drink from people, you're too good for that, I'm not going to feed the demons in your soul."

"But you'll feed your own?"

"I have control and my soul is already damaged, but I'll never let myself lose it."

"It's like you don't trust me." This was so frustrating, and I thought she could hear that in my voice.

"Of course I trust you, but not the demon inside." She vaguely wiggled her finger at my chest. At this point we kept having the same argument over and over, not one of us budging. I needed a break. I needed space. I got up and started packing a bag with essentials, and I could feel panic radiating off of her.

"I'm not mad, I think I just need some time away to think about everything, and about your offer," I clarified.

"Okay, whatever you need." She hugged me from behind and left the room, followed by the front door closing in the distance.

It wasn't like I had any money to book a hotel, or any friends I could reach out to who wouldn't bombard me with questions about my whereabouts and the events of the last month or so. Plus, I'd need to be able to have blood inconspicuously, so there was really only one place I could go.

Chapter Twenty-Six

Morana opened up the door, leaning seductively against the frame.

"No surprise that you've changed your mind." She smirked and I shot her a look. "You know I'm teasing, come in." She gestured for me to enter.

"Can I stay over? No funny business." I saw the menace leave her eyes, almost turning into something kind.

"Of course." She took my bag and led me up the stairs, where we both sat on the bed. "What happened?"

I proceeded to tell her that we had been arguing, but not what about, as I already knew what her opinion was. I told her about the offer she had made and how I felt about it. She actually listened and was taking it all in. I really refused to believe that she didn't have a soul, even if she were acting; selfish people wouldn't have the patience to listen, especially regarding someone they hate.

"And I just think I'll never be that good, or good enough, she puts me on this moral pedestal that I'd never be able to live up to." She grabbed both sides of my face and kissed me, causing fireworks. Something I had craved from the moment I met her, and it had finally been fulfilled, and, oh, was it worth the wait.

"Hannah, you are spectacular. " Although it was sudden, it was very gentle and almost loving, two things her persona claimed that she wasn't. "I won't let you think that about yourself, and if Araceli is making you feel that way, then she isn't treating you the way you deserve."

"I didn't think you *actually* felt this way, I thought you just wanted to mess with me."

"Hah, was my teasing not clear enough?" She smirked. "I could've let you kill that guy in the alleyway, but I actually pulled him away from you, because I knew you didn't want to – and also to note: right now would've been a great time to manipulate you into killing, which I haven't done and I could've let you and Araceli burn in the sunlight – I don't do these things for anyone. Only you, Hannah." She stared into my eyes before jumping up excitedly. "I've got a work event tomorrow—"

"Oh yeah, I can leave before that if you need." She took my hand and clasped both of hers around it.

"And I was going to say you should come with me, be my date?"

"Oh, okay, yes." She put her hand on my cheek and flashed a smile.

"Do you want me to sleep on the couch?" she asked while turning away. I squeezed her hand and pulled her back.

I went to bed on my side, facing outward. When she joined, she wrapped herself around my back, kissing the back of my neck, putting a leg between mine. Spooning me for the morning.

Chapter Twenty-Seven

I was woken up by her rubbing my neck. Standing over me.

"How do I keep waking up after everyone?" Was my instant reaction.

"Sleeping pattern, the change, eating habits, understandably your body is adjusting." She bent to the bottom drawer of a dresser pulling out a black box sealed with a bow, placing it in front of me on the bed. "For you." I opened it, inside was a sleek little yellow dress. "It'll fit perfectly." I looked up at her, a little confused.

"You haven't had time to go buy this." I raised my eyebrows. "How long have you had it?"

"Oh baby, I have a whole wardrobe for you." She winked and I scrunched up my face. "You want honesty, eh?"

"I like when you're honest."

"Who would I be if I didn't meet my girl's needs?" She played with my hair. "Since after that night in the police station" – I waved my hand in a roll to promote her to keep going on – "when I realised that maybe I wasn't interested in you because I wanted to mess with you, and it was more because I wanted to be around you." She let out a sigh. "There, are you happy?" My eyes welled, and all I could manage was a smile. "Although, you're still fun to tease." She winked.

"Thank you," I whispered.

I went into the ensuite to get changed and she spoke to me through the door.

75

"Have you been micro dosing?"

"No, she won't let me."

"Hmm, I'll bite my tongue."

"Thank you," I sang.

"You'll need to feed before we leave, I'll go sort something now." I heard her feet disappear down the stairs.

I stared at myself in the mirror, I've never owned clothing of this high a scale. Morana really does live like a rich bitch.

When I made it downstairs, I was greeted with:

"Oh what devastating beauty!" She hugged me. Behind her on the L couch was a man, as spread out as possible, taking up space. "If you want?" she asked. "I'll stop you, or we can figure out something else." I nervously nodded and she whispered, "He's a scammer, not a good guy." She walked behind him and I in front.

"Hey," he grunted, I could tell he thought he was being sexy. I climbed onto him on the couch and Morana pulled his head back by his hair, stretching out his neck. I looked at her for as long as I could before facing his neck, it felt like I was moving in slow motion, and like my body had taken over, I licked his neck and could feel his whole body tense, I bit in, the skin feeling like it just slid apart for my teeth, needing no effort at all. Morana rubbed the back of my neck as I drank.

"Okay, that's enough, my girl," she said gently and to my surprise I actually stopped, I was able to stop. I looked up at her and she pushed the hair out of my face. "Good job, babe." And then she finished him off. "Fuck, that was hot." She grabbed my hand. "Ready to go?"

As we got to the lobby, I realised it was still bright out. Outside the main doors sat a fully blacked out car at the end of the outdoor roof. Morana grabbed a large and deep umbrella covering both of our heads fully and we rushed into the back of the car, myself squeezing in first to find Merripen already in the end seat.

"Oh hey, your face is looking like it's healing well."

"Make up mostly."

"Oh, and in the alleyway, I didn't even notice you, you did a good job hiding the body."

"Yeah, you were too wrapped up in your own drama—"

"Merripen, I hope you aren't forgetting your place," Morana calmly chimed.

"Of course not, ma'am, my apologies."

"It's a few towns over, you can sleep on the journey and I'll wake you," she addressed me.

"What is it you do for work anyway?" I asked, resting my head on her shoulder.

"Ah, can't trust you with that information yet." Always teasing. She took my hand and I dozed off on her shoulder.

When she woke me up, it was dark out and the car had stopped. We stepped out into the lobby of a tall building, of which I couldn't quite tell if it was a hotel or a business building.

"You go ahead," she said to Merripen, who disappeared into a lift.

"Two rules: first, don't tell anyone that I'm nice, I thrive and succeed off of the fear I cause." She played with the strap of my dress. "Second, don't mention that you've never killed, it'll put you in danger."

"Danger? Like they'll hurt me?" She smiled letting air out of her nose.

"I wouldn't let anyone hurt you, no. But they'll make you kill there and then." She fixed my hair, I must've rustled it while sleeping. I leaned in to kiss her, hoping maybe it'd calm my nerves of the unknown and she pulled away. "I'll kiss you again once you do a good job today, and it'll be on your other lips, in between me spelling my name." She stuck her tongue out, everything inside me dropped, instantly losing any dryness from my panties. She had a menacing look in her eyes, I could tell she was excited because she knew she had sparked a reaction. Grabbing my hand, she took me to the lift in which she switched to a posher arm link. It went up twenty-seven floors before opening into an event area completely filled with windows on one side. Women scattered chatting everywhere, a band playing classical music tucked into a corner. And men lined up against the wall, who I could smell in the air.

"Humans?"

"Yes, but they know about us, so we can speak freely." A tall woman approached us greeting Morana with kisses on either side of her cheeks.

"You brought a guest?" She stared at me, head tilted.

"Yes, this is my Hannah." The woman gestured for my hand in hers, then snapped her head back at Morana, not letting go.

"Your, *your* Hannah? You didn't?" Morana rubbed the side of my neck while nodding happily. The woman put my chin in her hand and stepped closer really looking down onto my face, examining me. "She's rather beautiful, everyone will be ecstatic!" She dropped my head and took my hand again, I looked at Morana who gently rubbed my back to reassure me. The woman cleared her throat and the whole room came to a pause. "Morana has changed a human." She raised my hand up, nearly forcing me onto my toes. The room applauded and roared even louder than they had been before, she placed my hand into Morana's. "Congratulations, I'll leave you to it now."

"Was that your boss?" She snuffed at me.

"Babe, I'm the boss," she whispered in my ear. "People are going to be very curious about you, if you get uncomfortable later, just say and we'll leave." Another person approached us and put their hand out for a handshake with me, and before I lifted my hand she slapped theirs away. "If you're not allowed to touch me, what makes you think you're worthy of touching her?" She apologised profusely and backed away quickly. "Workplace Karen." She rolled her eyes. Throughout the night people came to talk to us, none of them addressing me, even when commenting about me. Some asked permission to shake my hand, but only asking Morana. The whole time she kept her arm across my back, her hand clutching my waist, squeezing me every so often. To be honest, it was probably better I didn't speak, as I didn't want to do anything wrong. Until we reached one woman.

"How are you adjusting?" I was a bit startled by the sudden acknowledgement, I had almost forgotten I even existed.

"Yeah, just getting used to the sleeping patterns."

"You know, I changed someone once."

"Really?" Morana sounded genuinely surprised.

"Yeah, some girl I grew up with actually, near enough instantly after I had been changed."

"Oh excuse me, I'll be right back." Morana slipped her arm away, and I had come to feel like it was a missing limb.

"Is she here?" Her eyes widened. "The girl you changed?"

"No, we parted ways, you see I was only a micro then and when I took the leap, she didn't agree, so I let her go off and do her own thing." She looked over at Morana. "But most makers aren't that kind." She looked like she was arguing with the people she was with, including Merripen. She came back over and returned her arm to where it had been perfectly.

"Excuse us, we must get going now."

"It was nice meeting you, Hannah." She was the only one that acknowledged me and treated me like a regular person and was also the only one Morana seemed less on edge around.

She led us through some back rooms, to a different lift than before, hidden in the back.

Chapter Twenty-Eight

She spoke when the doors closed.

"What have you been holding in all night?" I glanced at her, wondering if she was testing me, but I didn't think I could contain my thoughts much longer.

"Show dog."

"I know, I didn't expect them to become so comfortable, I'm sorry, new vampires aren't something that happen often any more and because you were changed by my hand, it's an even bigger deal."

"Thank you." She turned to look at me. "You put them in their place, and your presence was reassuring; you made me feel safe." She grabbed my lower back and pulled me into her kiss, we started making out, her turning me around and pushing my back to the side of the lift. We both moaned inside each other's mouths. In between breaths, she spoke to me.

"You done a great job..."

"Good girl."

"So much that I'm ready to fucking rip off that dress right now." She started rubbing my nipples, making them erect, the doors pinged open into an open room. "Take it off." I didn't think twice to even look around my surroundings, I was too caught up in the moment, she rubbed her hands against my skin and started kissing me again while walking backwards guiding me, stopping me with my back to a bed, my calves touching the mattress. "Remember the first time we were in bed together? It was life changing for you; tonight, will be no different." I could feel myself start to shake. "Lie down." By this point, I had turned into a puddle. She kissed from my lips to my boobs, taking off my bra, then down to my vag, ripping off my underwear with her teeth. Kissing my thighs and all around, even teasing me during sex. Until finally kissing me, sucking and licking, making me arch my back in pleasure and look up from the edge of the bed for the first time, only to see a human man standing in his boxers, staring across the room, trying not to look. The sight of him made me jump. She looked up at me. "Trust me?" I nodded. "Or do you want him to leave?" I just stared at her, not knowing how to even react, so she continued, easily making me forget about his existence.

Later, when we had moved up the bed, he had stuck his arm out to me and I then understood his reason for being there. I bit in drinking while lying down and being pleasured, spilling blood all over the place, which Morana happily licked off my body before taking his arm and drinking him dry then continuing on having her way with me.

I woke up and could see the sun rising out the window.

"Morning." Morana entered the room.

"The sunrise!" I panicked.

"Special windows, we're safe." She sat next to me on the bed and kissed me good morning, and, oh, was it a good morning. "I ran you a bath." She gestured towards a room behind a smudged window wall? The bath was a huge rectangle, too big for a bath but too little for a pool. Pink petals floated along the top of the water. I was still naked from the night before so went straight in, facing the windows to the outside so I could watch the sunrise. Morana sat out the side and started massaging my shoulders and I let out a groan, her touch absolutely electrified me.

"This is so nice."

"This is the life you could have—" I rolled my eyes.

"If I just killed?" She stopped and moved so I could see her face.

"No, you don't need to do what you don't want to, you never did." She sighed. "Still believe the worst in me, huh?"

"I'm sorry." I pushed the water around. "Why don't you join?" She took her robe off and came into the bath, moving me so that I was sitting on her and her back was on the edge. "Why didn't you let me return the favour last night?"

"You please me, I please you." She rubbed my neck with bathwater. "You did a good job at the event, so in return I gave you a good time, plus I wanted last night to be about you and it was still for both of us, I had an amazing time."

"Me too." She wrapped her arms around me.

"Do you know what your answer to her will be yet?" Morana was right in saying life with her would be much easier, and it wasn't like it was a case of breaking up with one to be with another, it was just choosing who to live with. I didn't know if I could live with taking advantage of someone who was suicidal, or the work that would entail, plus the hardships of needing to micro dose and Araceli not letting me.

"I don't know, I wouldn't even know what I'm supposed to do." She nuzzled her head into the back of mine, using my hair as a pillow.

"You know, I can work from pretty much anywhere, so if you moved with her and still wanted me nearby, I could find another ridiculous hotel to stay in." We both giggled.

I turned around to face her, still sitting on her, and kissed her, while she held my hips down. "Also, we can stay here as long as you want, and we can go back whenever you say."

I had decided to go home that day, even though I wasn't sure of my answer; I couldn't just leave Araceli hanging with no communication, it wasn't fair, even though I wanted so badly to spend more alone time with Morana, to get to know that side of her that no one else got to see.

The car pulled up at her hotel.

"I can get him to drive you to her?" I shook my head.

"I'll walk, she'd hate if you had access to her address."

"It's your address too, you know." Well, technically, it was Daniel's, but she had a point. But still, I didn't want to breach Daniel's privacy or Araceli's trust. She handed me a small box out of her purse. "It's a phone, so we can text?" I took it, at heart she was sensitive, but she didn't dare let anyone see that. She pulled me in for a long kiss goodbye and I wish we could've stayed in it forever. "Make sure she is worthy of you, okay?" I nodded. "To have you by her side makes her the most fulfilled person on this planet," she said rubbing my cheek, staring deep into my eyes. She started walking backward. "Text me?" She shrugged before heading off into the hotel.

Chapter Twenty-Nine

I returned to our home, which was empty when I arrived, so I decided to go to bed and rest.

I woke up to the front door closing. When I popped my head into the main room, I saw Daniel, the sight of me making him jump. He came over and gave me a hug, surprisingly, having him that close to me and I didn't want to kill him? I think it was the micro dosing that was adding to my tolerance. He told me that Araceli was out, but he didn't know where.

"So, are you really doing better?" I was blunt.

"I guess, the thoughts aren't so loud any more, but they never really go away." He nodded at himself. "So you don't need to worry about me any more, I've kind of adapted my thought process to make sure I don't get in the bads again." He shot me a thumbs up. "I'm happy for you guys to stay as long as you need, but you don't need to stay on my behalf any more." It was good, in the way that Daniel believed that Araceli was helping him, and how she did too. But I couldn't shake the back of my mind telling me it was a saviour complex, but I didn't want to believe in negatives when the outcomes were positive.

Araceli came back home, covered in sweat.

"Hey," she grunted.

"I missed you!" I moved in for a hug.

"You did?" We pecked each other on the lips. "I missed you too, Han."

"What have you been doing?" I glared at the sweat on her

head.

"Exercise, where did you go?" She wiped her head. "Actually, I don't need to know." I grabbed her hand.

"It's okay, I was with Morana." She didn't react. "I'm sorry, I know it's not what you want to hear."

"Figured." She took her shirt off. "So are you two a thing now?"

"I mean, I guess we're kind of dating, yeah." She huffed. "You said it was okay to be open."

"Yeah, it is." She put her hand on my shoulder, looking down at my face. "I can't stop you from seeing her, are you sure you can trust her?" I nodded. "But I don't want to hear about her." She set the boundary.

"And I need you to accept that I'll be micro dosing." She rolled her index finger along the top of her nose.

"So, I take it you've already started?" she assumed. "When did you start micro dosing?"

"In the alleyway."

"And you didn't tell me?"

"Because you'd think it was her fault, and it wasn't, she helped me, she *is* helping me."

"And I'm not?"

"You both help me in your own ways." I cuddled into her but she kept her arms still. "This is one of the good points of non-monogamy, you can get everything you need from different people, and spread the most happiness and love, without putting a tonne of impossible pressure and expectations on one person." She rested her chin on my head, which I took as her giving in. "So in regards to me, you two are a team." Morana's teasing had rubbed off a little.

"That's not funny." She gently pushed me away. "You know

how I feel about it affecting your soul and she doesn't care—"

"No, you have different beliefs and that's okay," I cut her off mid rant. A rant I'd heard far too often within the little time we'd been together, already falling into elderly couple routine.

"What about my question?" She changed the subject.

"I don't know, I still need time to think, what if we stayed here another month and we can figure it out?" Her expression said she wasn't happy with that, but she'd never actually admit it.

"Eh, I don't want to take advantage of Daniel." Keep your mouth shut, Hannah, no comment, no negative thoughts, leave it be – now is not the time to start other fights. "But I'll talk to him, for you." She put her arms around my waist. "Because I'm committed to having this life with you."

Chapter Thirty

I was woken up by the phone buzzing on the bedside table, without looking at the screen, I answered.

"Hello?" Araceli rolled over in the bed.

"What the fuck is that?"

"Has she never seen a phone before?" Morana scoffed. I walked out of the room. "What are you doing tonight?"

"Nothing planned."

"Dinner date? At mine?"

I arrived at Morana's that night. She was wearing a green suit with a black trim and no top (of course). She handed me a collection of tulips when answering the door.

"For you." She kissed me on the lips and rubbed both my arms.

She led me through the room by hand. "I would've taken you to dine out but—"

"Yeah not very possible ha."

"Actually, in bigger cities we have clubs we can be free at." Morana had a whole other world waiting outside of this shithole, yet she stayed here for me.

"So there'd be humans like there were at your work event?"

"Yeah, but only the most powerful are allowed to kill, to save staff turnover." She smirked.

"And they'd know? How do they recruit humans that are willing to do that?"

"Some humans are obsessed with vampires because of the

shitty fantasy media tropes, so when they find out we're real they want to serve us in hopes we'll change them." She tutted. "Some are just kinky and into it, others have no regard for their wellbeing, and then there's always those who are desperate and will do anything to get by, the pool really is endless."

"And that's the same way you get humans at your work? Is your company all vampires?"

"Yeah, we can work from home during the sunlight and do our own thing come nightfall, otherwise we'd have to get night jobs and be around the humans with no time to feed, and it'd likely be low paying jobs, really what's the point in living forever if it's only going to be mediocre?" A knock on the door interrupted her. "That must be our takeaway!" She winked. Another man entered her hotel room of his own will, only to not leave. She assured me before we fed that she tried to pick out only bad men when I was involved. Once we had finished our 'meal', we sat on the couch and continued to chat.

"So, any verdict about the Araceli thing?" I told her that we were staying for another month for me to decide, but that she was clearly unhappy about it. "You shouldn't need to change or deny yourself for someone else, Hannah."

"Isn't that what you're doing for me? Accepting I won't kill?"

"I don't *need* to do that though; I want to, and I've been perfectly clear about my opinion on it." She squeezed my shoulder. "I have never seen someone show so much self-control, so much strength," she said climbing onto my lap, "your dedication to it almost convinces me to change my mind." She laughed at the absurd thought. "I never thought I'd feel anything like this, that I'd ever want something more than I want blood, but here you are and I'm so in love with you." My heart melted.

Such beautiful words that I didn't deserve and I could tell were difficult but exciting for her to admit. "So, does Araceli get all the glory or would I also be able to have the honour of calling you my girlfriend?"

"I love you too, Morana, so yes, I'd love to be your girlfriend." She shrieked happily and we had a long kiss to seal the deal. I squeezed her hips happily and she flinched.

"Oooh."

"What's wrong?" She shook her head.

"Don't bother with it," she said pulling her blazer over, but I insisted, pushing it open to see a large bruise on her side making me gasp. She tilted my head up to look at her face. "It's okay, please don't worry."

We only cuddled that night, but it was still so intimate.

Chapter Thirty-One

It was a rough adjustment over a few weeks but we were trying to get into a routine of me staying with Morana and feeding one night, and staying with Araceli without the next.

One night, Araceli gave in to her curiosity.

"So, what exactly do you do when micro dosing with her?"

"Oh, I just drink from them and she finishes them."

"So, she kills them, and you let it happen?" She pulled a face, trying her hardest not to judge before knowing all the information. "What's the point in not killing if you're just going to stand by and watch someone else kill?"

"Well, they'd probably die anyway, so she's just making sure that it isn't me that pulls the plug," I rationalised.

"So, you drink them close to death?"

"Eh, I guess, but I don't kill them," I clarified.

"Han, that's not micro dosing." I scrunched up my face at her, she's so judgemental. "What I do with Daniel is take enough to get me by, but not enough to hurt him or make him ill, he's never close to death." She squished the bridge of her nose so tightly that I thought it was going to explode, her eyes started to water. *"Fuck."* She knocked her fist gently against the counter. "I—" she was interrupted by my phone ringing, she huffed. "Answer it." I was hesitant taking it out of my pocket. "Answer the fucking phone."

"Hey, Emi is coming through for some business tonight, I thought it'd be nice for the three of us to hang out again, if you're free of course."

"Emi?"

"Yeah, the one that was actually nice to you at the event."

"Oh yeah sure, I'd love to get to know more people in your life!"

"Brilliant, I'll see you later, babe."

"What did you say?" She shook her head. "Actually, never mind, back to what I was saying." She took a deep breath. "I don't know if I can be with you any more." The words came at me like a slap, causing a shock through my body. My brain really could not connect the dots on this one.

"Wait, *WHAT?*" Although we bickered, we never fought so much that it should be a worry.

"Just go out and see your girlfriend."

"No, obviously I'm going to stay here and talk with you."

"Hannah, I want you to leave – I need time to think, please."

Chapter Thirty-Two

"Hello!" Morana greeted me with a kiss on the cheek.

"Is your friend here?" I blankly rolled into the room.

"No, not yet, are you okay? You seem spaced." She guided me by the hips to the couch.

"I think Araceli just broke up with me?" She snapped off her seat.

"WHAT? What an idiot! Want me to go tell her off? Or I have people I can send to torment her." I shook my head, I didn't even doubt that she did have people on hand for that sort of thing. "I know for a fact you could get any vampire you wanted, and I'll be your wing-woman, or wing-girlfriend? Fuck Araceli." I could tell she was angry, but she tried her best to be sensitive instead. "Shit, want me to tell Emi not to come?"

"No, it's fine, let's have a fun night. I'm not upset, just surprised I guess." She kissed the top of my head. "At least I won't be getting constantly judged any more." I shrugged.

"I love you." She looked into my eyes, trying to read me. "Upstairs, I have an outfit for you." Just then the door was knocked and I ran upstairs to get ready while Morana answered.

Coming back downstairs to them standing over a coffee table, Emi took my hands and kissed both my cheeks.

"Nice to see you again, you look gorgeous this evening."

"A real heart stealer, Emi." Morana slid her arm around my back, squeezing my waist and kissing me on the cheek. "Should we go to the club tonight? Show the humans how to dance, maybe take home a meal?" Before anyone could answer, the door rattled, being beaten on repeat. "Or maybe, with manners like that, we can start dining now," she added before answering the door. As soon as she twisted the handle the door was thrown open from the other side, Araceli storming through. "Way to make an entrance! Here for more?" Morana rubbed where she had been bruised before and I realised that it was Araceli that had caused it.

"*You*, shut the fuck up." She waved her fist in her face, Morana refusing to even flinch. She turned and looked in my direction. "I needed to see. If. It. Was. True." she spoke slowly, as if she had seen something the rest of us hadn't.

"For someone so against killing and violence, you really are quick to jump to threatening people." Morana chose to provoke her further with her teasing. Araceli only grunted, clearly agitated but not bothering to give her a reply. She stared in our direction, but instead of at me she burned her eyes through Emi. I moved down the room, I wanted to diffuse the situation, but was also furious that she was so rude, and intruding Morana's space and threatening her.

"What are you doing here anyway? *YOU* broke up with me, remember?" I tried to say quietly so Emi didn't hear.

"I didn't break up with you," she announced for her audience.

"*What?*" I spat. She started to square up to Morana. "Okay, well I'm breaking up with you now, come on, get out," I said nudging her to leave. Not my finest moment, but I'd seen what damage she could cause to people when she was angry, and all I wanted was for her to leave so that everyone was safe. She looked me in the eyes, hers glistened with water, clearly hurt. I obviously hadn't learned from breaking up with Dominic, in such a similar blunt and hurtful way, but the way I saw it, it was necessity to get what was needed in each moment.

"Fine," she huffed. "I refuse to be with a killer anyway; you can't cheat the system."

"Are you delusional?" How could she think that? What was it with the people I loved, not really knowing me at all? First Dominic is quick to think I'm a drug addict and now Araceli is accusing me of being a killer, and even when we were together, she had this solid idea of me being more morally set than I am, she wanted me to be her. This made the breakup so much easier than it should've been.

"You have been bringing people close to death; you're a fucking killer, Han, you're past saving; you're basically one of them." She gestured to the other ladies of the room.

"Nah, you're not coming in here and disrespecting Hannah like that, don't talk to her if you can't respect her." Morana jumped to my defence.

"And YOU," she addressed Morana only, "I bet you manipulated Emi just like you're doing to Han."

"Wow! We didn't even know Morana then!" Morana and I snapped our heads at Emi, both confused that they knew each other. "Such a drama queen, Araceli, all these years and you still haven't let go nor have you changed." She walked in front of me, almost putting her body in the way as a guard. "I made the choice, and you didn't, and when you didn't, you decided that me having killed was unacceptable and that you didn't want me in your life, as with that now; no one currently wants you here so what is the point in starting fights?"

"Wait, you told me your maker died in the turf war!" I clicked. Emi looked at me then chuckled.

"Is that the story you've been telling? Pathetic that you can't even tell the truth, that you're alone by choice, rather than being tortured like you pretend." She pushed her away from Morana. She made a crater in the door from the shape of her fist before leaving in a hurry, not looking at anyone.

"Strange." Morana mimicked dusting off her shoulders while Emi closed the door.

"You dated her as well?" I nodded. "You're tougher than I thought." She laughed. "She takes patience." She raised her eyebrows. "Are you okay though?"

"Yeah, I'm just glad she didn't start a fight."

"You think the three of us couldn't have taken her on?" Morana flexed. "So you're the one to thank for bringing that nuisance into our lives?" Emi raised her hands in a surrender.

"I was naive once." She threw her hand into a flop. "She wasn't any easier for me to deal with over the years."

The three of us shrugged off the event and decided to stay in instead. Swapping stories and laughing. Emi told us the true story of how Araceli was alright in the beginning until one day flicking a switch, cutting off all their vampire friends, claiming they were evil, and that her and Emi were the only good ones in the world. Emi mocked the co-dependency of it, but stated that she didn't see clearly then because she thought she loved Araceli. She said how she convinced the micro dosers to become sort of vigilantes against the feeders and how Emi had had enough and killed for the first time due to the stress Araceli had caused, causing her to be disowned and villainised.

I could tell Emi was the closest thing to a friend to Morana in her work, whereas everyone else was an employee or a nuisance, and I think tonight gave her the opportunity to be more free, more herself around Emi.

"When I met you, I got the sense that you hadn't killed and

could feel there wasn't that sort of ownership energy you mostly find with makers and their bitten." She looked from me to Morana. "But I didn't want to cramp your status by even thinking about it too much, got to have the staff in fear." She winked at Morana. She leaned over the table and touched my face. "No wonder you have all these people fussing over you, not just your beauty, but even your personality and strength in the short time I've known you shining through."

"Why don't you two kiss already?" Morana smiled. We both looked at her and she nodded as if to say 'go on'. Emi looked at me, hand still on my face and I leaned in kissing her, knowing Morana was watching. I took her hand and walked her round to Morana, then taking her hand in my other, leading them both upstairs. I sat on the bed and nodded at them, for them to start kissing.

I couldn't help but wonder if I was doing this to piss off Araceli, but quickly deleted the idea, because I was definitely doing it for my own pleasure. After all, it's an all-female threesome, who doesn't dream of that?

The three of us got undressed. Morana sat behind me taking my hair down from its tie, her body working as my back rest, kissing me on the neck while Emi started on her knees at the edge of the bed. They each grabbed one of my boobs. Emi started licking, long, slow strokes making sure to stimulate everywhere she could, starting to flick. I lay back on top of Morana who was touching my body with her soft hands.

"She's delicious." She stuck her arm out for Morana to take her hand and walk round. "Your taste." She guided her towards were she was just sat, swapping places. Emi pushed me back down on the bed kissing me then sitting on my face.

Chapter Thirty Three

Emi stayed until the next evening, the three of us well filling the time in bed together. I couldn't even say it was an unforgettable night, because it was much longer than a night.

When we were alone again, I talked about working for Morana if I ever got to know what it was that she actually did.

"You don't have to, what's mine is yours." She gestured to the whole room. "Plus I wouldn't want either of us to worry about you being safe regarding your eating habits." She ran her thumb across my palm. "But if you get bored and want to, of course, you can work with me."

I had the opportunity to live the pampered life that most people dreamed of, but never came close to achieving. Honestly after the illness, stress and fighting over the last two months, it was a welcome thought, for now. To have a bit of ease and rest, and no doubts – a tonne of pleasure.

Upon reflection, I think Araceli's love for me was conditional, but only because she expected me to be (or thought I was) someone else. I was still pissed off about the rage she had, and how she let it drive her at times. But I also still wanted to talk to her, make things more amicable, because no one deserves a horrible split, plus what if we were to run into each other in the future, or what if she didn't let go like she refused to do with Emi?

Morana made it clear that there was no rush and that it was up to me when we left town and where we went. We had arranged to leave within a few weeks' time, and that I'd drop by Daniel's to try and speak to Araceli before I left. I let Morana decide where we were going, as I had no idea what else the world, or the vampire world, had, but it was exciting to think about somewhere that wasn't that hotel room, although plenty of fun was had there.

Chapter Thirty-Four

Our last time waking up in the hotel and I woke up with no one beside me. The night before I had gone to Daniel's only to find that Araceli was long gone.

I travelled downstairs to see if Morana was home, only to walk in on a whole scene. Morana was handcuffed to the railing of the staircase. Dominic sat zoned out on a dining chair parked in front of her.

"Oh, you're here! Great, let's get started!" Merripen seemed to appear out of nowhere.

"Shut up and unlock me now!" Morana was firm, stern. Merripen kicked the back of the seat.

"Get up." Dominic stumbled onto his feet and she threw the chair on its side.

"Stop, you're not doing this." Morana was angry, but she kept her tone commanding.

"I've worked for you for forty years; I'm not going to let you be seen as weak for having a soft spot for this child that doesn't have the clit to kill." I had never heard her speak so much, but it made sense why Morana didn't let her talk. "You've not worked as hard as you have to let your name be tarnished over *feelings.*" She shivered.

"Come on, let me show you out." I started to approach Dom.

"No, no, no, no." She pulled out a knife. "Today, you're getting your first kill." She darted her eyes from him to me. "Unless you want to die instead? Either way, it removes an obstacle." She shrugged. "I had to flirt with him the last three hours to get him here, and he's *so painfully boring,*" she actually said this with pain. "How did you deal with him for so many years?" She put her hand up to say stop. "To be fair, you're pretty uninteresting too, everyone just loves you because you're... new." Rude, but correct, I really didn't deserve any of the love I'd received in recent months. I turned to look at Morana and she shook her head.

"If you uncuff me now, I may consider not killing you." Merripen took a step closer to Dominic who was in too much of a shock to even seem present. "Red headed fuck." Although her words were angry, Morana's tone was still calm and posh, although I knew deep down she was enraged, and that her threat of murder was very real.

"Why don't you put the knife away? I'm sure being boring would make Dominic suffer more than dying would, think of the years of unhappiness over the moments of pain." She rolled her eyes and slapped her arms at her sides.

"I'm not here to make him suffer, I don't give a fuck about a human – I'm here for you to grow up and stop sacrificing our livelihood," she groaned. "Fuck's sake, woman, do you need me to tie your laces for you?" She thrust the knife into his shoulder rushing it straight back out causing blood to squirt and pour everywhere. I could see his body start to sway as if he were about to faint and I moved in and caught him, the wound landing right under my mouth.

"*HANNAH.*" I heard unrecognisable panic that didn't belong in Morana's voice. "You don't need to do it." I could tell they were both talking, but it all turned to vague mumbles. I took a deep breath in letting the smell consume me, I stared into Morana's eyes and tried to tell her it was okay, it was natural, who I was. I turned my head to face the wound, licking what I could from it before moving up to the neck to make my mark, the last mark.

I dropped to the floor, legs crossed in a basket, Dominic's body flopping to the ground beside me, almost in slow motion. My eyes blurred and all the colours in front of me merged together like a Van Gogh. I couldn't hear a thing. I could see a bunch of movement in front of me, red splashes going off like fireworks. A huge weight floated off my shoulders. I felt my brain melting away, like I was now in the back seat and someone had taken the steering wheel away from me and it felt good, it felt so fucking good.